# Mail Order Bride

# A Bride for Mackenzie

Sun River Brides
Book 2

Karla Gracey

First Printing, 2016

# Dedication

I dedicate this book to my mother, as she was the one who kept urging me to write, and without her enthusiasm I would never of written and published my books.

# Contents

# Chapter One

"Annie, I need my reticule. Do you know where I left it when we came in from the recital?" Carolynn yelled angrily. Annie sighed. The girl could be all elegance when she wanted, yet as soon as her parents were out of the house, out came the hoyden and made a perfectly turned out young woman appear more coarse than a common fishwife.

"Miss Carolynn, why not try retracing your steps?" Annie replied patiently. There was no point in trying to reason with her once she was in high dudgeon, even though apparently this was her job until a new governess could be found for the two girls. She was simply too tired, and had too much to get done to get involved in Miss Caro's petty concerns today. Mr and Mrs Hepworth had only just come into their money. Mr Hepworth had made a lot of money selling hardware to miners, and they liked to show it off in any way they could. But that meant a lot of useless trinkets and too much furniture and it was always down to Annie to make sure that the house looked as immaculate as possible. The sad thing was that they simply didn't understand that buying everything new, and at the highest possible price, did not convey the appearance they longed to portray. It just made their home cluttered and made for more cleaning for their poor overworked staff.

"But however can I do that? I cannot go to the theatre alone and just walk back now can I," the young woman added sarcastically. She was about to turn fifteen, and believed she was cleverer than anyone older or younger than herself. Annie was sure the phase would pass and the sweet girl she had once been would return, but it was proving hard to tolerate while she continued to have these tantrums over nothing. With a sigh she put down the silver coffee pot she had been polishing and tucked her cloth securely into her apron.

"Come now, you will surely find it faster than I Miss Carolynn," she added as she reluctantly bustled into the hallway to try and calm the young woman. "Ask Miss Margaret to help you to search. Your Mother and Father will not be best pleased if I haven't finished the silver in time for their supper party tonight after all."

Annie had prayed over and over since her dear friend, Myra Gilbert, had left for Montana to become the bride of Carlton Green that a new governess would be found soon. Trying to keep up with the two girls and her chores was leaving her worn to the nub. She was sure she hadn't enjoyed a quiet moment in weeks. Though the girls could be kind, and very sweet at times, they interrupted her all the time and that meant she got the telling off from her employer that her usual tasks were either not done, or not up to her usual standard. Mrs Hepworth in particular simply didn't seem to understand that doing two jobs that both needed a person's fullest attention would mean that corners somewhere had to be cut.

She turned her back and went back into the dining room and the seemingly endless task ahead of her, praying that Miss Carolynn would stop bothering her over something so trivial when she had so much still to do. But sadly, the young woman followed her. "But Annie, it has my letter from Myra in it. I would have thought that you would be as eager as I to hear news of how she is faring in Montana," she said slyly as she appeared in the doorway. She was a dear thing, but lazy as a cat in the sunshine.

Myra hadn't let her get away with it, and neither would Annie. She simply didn't have the time.

"I have my own letter Miss Carolynn, and I shall enjoy reading it when I have finished my work. I don't know how you ever intend to keep a husband young lady. You simply don't seem to understand that there is work to be done before you can play. Miss Myra would be heartbroken to think that all her lessons and her hard work had been so easily forgotten." Even Annie could hear the uncharacteristic exasperation in her voice, and Carolynn flushed with shame.

"You are right. She would extol the virtues of assisting you as much as we can, and to be self sufficient. But she isn't here is she?" Annie gave her a stern look. "Oh Annie, you can't blame me for at least trying to take advantage of the absence of a governess. Who knows what kind of dragon Papa will appoint next!"

"If he did employ someone a little stricter it would be for your own good."

"I know, I know. I am sorry, honestly. Is there anything we can do to help, dear Annie?" she said, moving towards the vast dining table, her doe eyes imploring Annie to forgive.

"Pick up a rag and polish everything you can see 'til it shines," Annie said with a smile, not expecting the girl to actually do an ounce of work, but it had been good of her to at least offer her assistance.

"Margaret? Come down. Annie needs a hand. Stop being such a lazy puss!" Carolynn called to her sister, leaving Annie open-mouthed. A younger, and quieter version of Caro appeared, book in hand. She put it down without a murmur of complaint, and both girls picked up their cloths and began to copy Annie's example. Annie smiled at them kindly.

The girls really weren't so bad, they just needed a little reminder every now and again of how to behave and to think of others every once in a while. Myra had told her just that as they had said their goodbyes, when the clever governess had been whisked off to the wilds of Montana by her handsome and dashing farmer. Annie couldn't help it, she had dreamed of something similar happening to her for weeks after their departure. But, she was just a chamber maid. Romance wasn't for the likes of her. She took her frustrations out on her work, and there was never a single bit of the house that wasn't spotlessly clean because of it.

The afternoon passed swiftly. The girls were excellent company, and they worked hard. When they stood back to admire their work all three young women put their hands on their hips and sighed contentedly. Annie chuckled. "Thank you," she said as they admired their gleaming work together.

"However do you do it, day in and day out Annie? I am quite fagged and we have done barely half the amount you did," Carolynn said in admiration.

"I'm used to it I suppose, and don't say 'fagged'! Your Mother would have the vapors if she heard you."

"What she doesn't know won't hurt her. And she would have the vapors if she heard you say such a thing of her too Annie! Now, may I please take Margaret and go in search of my reticule now?"

"Of course," Annie said with a grin.

"It is in your room, on your bed," Margaret said with an exasperated look. "You really are quite stupid sometimes." Carolynn looked at her, her brown eyes flashing in her sudden fury.

"You could have told me!"

"That wouldn't have been half as much fun. And, you didn't think to ask!"

"Get on with you, leave me to my work. I have a lot to do before tonight," Annie said ushering them out of the room. "Get up to your room, and stay there. I'll be up around six with the water for your baths; I shall be so glad when your Papa finishes getting the house fully plumbed and I can save my poor aching back! Remember your Mother will expect you both to be clean and presentable when the Montagues arrive."

"Yes Annie, of course Annie," they chorused as they raced up the grand staircase before she could scold them further.

Annie looked over the silverware. It was good. She wouldn't have to redo a single piece. Her day suddenly felt so much lighter, a task that usually took four hours had been completed in just two – she may even get to stop and rest for a few minutes before supper after all. Swiftly she fetched her brushes and the big tin of beeswax polish and began to sweep and dust the grand dining room, the drawing room and the library. She had already ensured that the grand hallway and the water closets were all sparkling before she had accompanied the girls to the recital at the Opera House. She hummed as she worked, a tune she had picked up whilst there. She had never been in a box before, and it had been a shock to her how luxurious it was in comparison to the gallery at the very top of the theatre that she occasionally managed to save enough to purchase a standing ticket for.

When she had completed her tasks she glanced at the large grandfather clock in the hallway, and was pleased to see it was only five o'clock. She still had an entire hour before she had to assist the girls to get ready, and her final task of the day was simply to lay the table. She would have a full forty minutes to herself if she was lucky. She moved with haste to the china cupboard. They would be using the Lenox chinaware this evening. It was brand new, and very delicate. She and Cook had been almost nervous as they had unpacked it and washed and dried it carefully before putting it away. She took each plate carefully between her fingers, placing it delicately on each setting. She wiped the crystal glasses carefully as she put each one in place, and gave each piece of cutlery a final polish as she laid it in place. Glancing over the table with her practiced eye, she wandered slowly round the table, nudging and tweaking until everything was perfect.

The clock chimed for the quarter hour, and Annie grinned. She had achieved perfection in record time. Praising herself she headed downstairs to the kitchen and her rocking chair by the fire. She would put her feet up, read the newspaper and her letter from Myra. It would be wonderful to know how she was doing, and if she was still as happy as she had been the day she set off on her big adventure. Annie hoped so. She had been a good friend, and she deserved a good life.

The kitchen was abuzz, Cook had hired in a couple of ladies from her church to help her. The three of them were up to their elbows in flour, pies, and vegetables. It felt wrong to sit and rest her weary bones while they rushed around, so Annie grabbed a newspaper from the rack and headed upstairs to her room. It wasn't much, but she did at least get to keep it all to herself. She looked around at the sparse furnishings, and was grateful she lived so simply. When you spent your life cleaning up after others – especially those with so many beautiful things that needed such special care, having nothing but a bed and a chest of drawers was restful.

She threw herself face down onto her mattress, and lay propped up on her elbows. She read Myra's letter first. It was short but she was clearly happy in Montana, and couldn't' seem to stop extolling the virtues of her handsome farmer. Annie felt a pang of jealousy as she read her words. It all seemed to happen so quickly, so simply. But she was sure that not every woman who set off into the West in search of love was so lucky. Annie missed her terribly, and she longed to have a husband and a home of her own. She was tired of always caring for everyone else but herself.

She put the letter down, and picked up the newspaper. Quickly she flicked through the pages to the Society section. She loved to read about all the gossip and scandal. She knew she shouldn't, but living vicariously through others was her only real pleasure in life. She was simply too tired by the time she finished her work each day to go out and be sociable, though it did mean that her nest egg of savings was growing safely and securely. She gasped as she read about her favorite actress being found in a hotel suite with a ridiculously wealthy banker, and about the opera singer who prided himself on being a family man being found in flagrante with one of the corps de ballet. To have such free time to make such foolish mistakes made her chuckle to herself. It was oddly reassuring to know that having wealth and fame did not necessarily make your life any happier – or make you even a jot wiser than those who served you.

She thumbed through the rest of the pages, wondering if anything else might catch her eye. She didn't much care for the news; it was too often full of tragedy and horror for her liking. But occasionally she would find a story that gave a little ray of hope and stoked her faith in the goodness of people. Sadly, there seemed to be little of such interest today, yet she stopped suddenly when she reached a page she had not seen in the Boston Globe before - a page of Matrimonial advertisements. She couldn't stop herself, her curiosity was piqued. She began to read, and was surprised at how many were actually from lonely women. She wouldn't have thought any woman would be so desperate as to degrade herself in such a way in front of the entire world.

The greater majority of the advertisements were from men though, and from all over the country, even some here in Boston. Clearly finding a bride in such a way was becoming so common place that people weren't just using it as a last resort. She wondered if any of them truly was as wonderful as their carefully chosen words made out - not one seemed to ring true to her. If they truly were such paragons, finding a wife should surely be no difficulty at all? But one simply worded advertisement made her stop and smile, a warm sense of connection settling over her in a way that felt like she was coming home.

> *A Gentleman of Montana, seeks a woman with a view to Matrimony. She should be polite and kind, and be able to make of his house a home. His needs are few, and his wealth not extraordinary, but there is enough to support us both and for us to consider a family some day. The subscriber is a man of simple tastes. All responses to Box 378, Boston Globe.*

He sounded like her. She didn't need much in life. But, she did want a home and a family. Myra had been lucky, why couldn't she be as content with a match made in this way? Didn't she deserve to have something of her own? Hadn't she spent enough of her life alone? Surely she had more than made up for her mistakes by now and was due some kind of happiness? Maybe the gentleman might live near to Sun River and she would be able to visit with her friend? Eagerly, recklessly she penned a response and wondered if she had lost her wits as she rushed out of the house to mail it before she had to return to her duties, and the dull and uneventful life she knew she deserved.

# Chapter Two

*Dear Gentleman of Montana,*

*Good day to you, I pray this finds you in good health. I do not know exactly what to say, so please forgive me if my words seem stilted or even rushed. I have never done anything so impetuous as to contact you in my entire life. I don't even know what possessed me to put pen to paper and write, but I just felt the strangest urge that I should regret it if I did not do so.*

*I am a chambermaid, and I live and work in a big house in Boston for a lovely family. I have been working extra hard recently as a friend left to get married and she has not yet been replaced. I have some education, but not sufficient to be a governess to two young women who already outstrip me in their knowledge. Yet, I try my best to at least teach them useful skills and try to keep them to their studies in comportment and manners.*

*I cannot say I enjoy being a maid, but I do get an immense sense of pleasure from seeing a job well done. I am a quiet sort, love reading when I have the time. But I am happiest when I am busy and have plenty to keep me occupied. I should very much like to correspond with you, to get to know you with a view to seeing if we might suit. I should very much like to be mistress of a home I could make with a supportive partner, and to become a mother someday.*

*Please tell me of yourself, I should love to hear of your home and what you do. Do you enjoy music and the theatre, or are you a homebody happy to curl up with a good book and a warm fire at the end of the day?*

*I look forward to your response, though I am sure you will receive many replies from women far more interesting than myself. I shall understand if I hear nothing further.*

*Yours most hopefully*

*Annie Cahill*

Mack put the simple little letter down on the left hand side of his large oak desk. He looked at the towering pile on the right. It surprised him how so many of the women who had replied to his advertisement had not asked a single thing about him. Annie Cahill was the only one so far who had not only wanted to know more of his life, but had even asked after his wellbeing.

He could not explain it, even to himself, but something about her short missive made him feel comfortable and content. He was no fool; he knew that feeling passion for a woman one met through an advertisement in the newspaper was not ever going to be likely, but he did at least want to not feel revulsion towards the woman he wrote to, maybe considered bringing here, to Montana, to be his bride. As he looked over the other responses once more, looking for any hint of kindness, humility or even simple politeness he could find nothing. He threw them on the fire, and stared again at the plain spoken words of Annie Cahill. This quiet and unassuming woman intrigued him. She had told him little of herself, and he was sure it was not because there was little to know - but because she believed her life to be of little interest. That in itself put her head and shoulders above the vapid and vain women whose letters were now crisping and crackling up in the flames.

He leaned back in his chair, and ran his fingers through his hair.

The ends curled as they reached his collar, reminding him he really needed to get a haircut. He rubbed his hands over his heavily stubbled cheeks; it had definitely been too long since he had visited the barbers. Mack looked out at the sheeting rain and decided that he would take a trip into Great Falls, he would get nothing done out on the land in weather such as this. It had been stormy for days and he was beginning to feel confined. His place was out on the land herding his cattle – but even he knew better than to do much more than check on them once or twice a day when thunder, lightning and wind raged outside. He couldn't afford to get sick and so he had learned to temper his naturally adventurous side – his sister called it recklessness and she was probably right.

"Mackenzie if you are going to be under my feet like this, you could at the very least clean up after yourself," Penelope's voice called down the stairs. Mack listened to her steps, the wooden floorboards creaking as she made her way towards the cozy little room he used as an office. "Anyone worth responding to today?" she asked him, her tone a little more kindly.

"Just the one." He handed over the letter. Penelope read it in silence, but a smile began to play around her lips as she did so.

"She sounds lovely – what little she has given away." She looked back at the address. "She's from Boston, and the governess at her place of work has just left - I wonder if she knows Myra Green," she mused. Mack looked at her confusion knotting his brow.

"Why ever should she know Mrs Green?"

"Because Mrs Green was once Miss Gilbert, and because she was a governess in Boston until very recently! Do you not ever listen to a word anyone tells you dear brother?"

"Not such things as that, no! I just knew Carlton looks like the cat that got the cream since he brought her home. It is good to see him happy. He works too hard, and has no help."

"Well he does now - and he's hired Ted Holkham and young Eric Graham. He should find things much easier now."

"And a pretty wife to keep his home and make him fat. Sounds like bliss," Mack joked, but he couldn't deny that a small part of him was more than a little jealous of his friend. He had gotten lucky.

"I know you'll never admit that you would miss me if I weren't here, but one day I shall be married and out of your hair, and then you will regret not having taken a wife," Penelope said poking her tongue out at him.

"I know, and that is why I agreed to let you put that blasted advertisement in the newspaper in the first place. Now, I have found one woman out of too many to count that I would consider writing to I thought you would be happy."

"I am, and I shall tell Callum that finally there may be hope that we can wed and I can leave you to your own devices!"

"I have told you a hundred times dear sister; do not put off your nuptials just for me. He is a good man, he won't wait forever – no matter how besotted he is with you right now. You're not getting any younger after all," he teased. "I shall be fine, can take care of myself you know."

"If I left you for even five minutes you would burn your supper and the house down." She patted him affectionately on the cheek.

"Well, maybe Miss Annie will be able to come and take care of me and you will be free to burn Callum's toast every morning instead of mine!"

"Ha, ha! What are you doing today? Please tell me you will be getting out from under my feet you pest?"

"You'd send me out in that?" he asked incredulously, a grin tweaking at the corners of his mouth. "Don't fret. I shall be out of your hair. I am going to take a little trip into Great Falls. I need to go to the bank and discuss my plans for the herd. I may even stay overnight, take in a show, go to the barbers and get a good shave and trim. I may even pop by the station to find out how much passage to Boston on the train would cost."

"That sounds hopeful, and after only one letter too," Penelope said smiling, but Mack could see her brain working. She knew him too well, knew that he had found something in this young woman's words that had touched him and made him curious.

His curiosity had done them both a lot of favors over the years. Without it they would not have made the move here, and would not have taken the chance to become ranchers. His curiosity about their neighbor, Callum Walters, had also paid off handsomely. The quiet man had kept himself to himself upon his arrival in Sun River, but the perfectly tended fields full of handsome and hardy horses and his immaculate fencing had intrigued Mack. He had to know who was capable of such precision – especially as he was out there doing it alone. The moment the reclusive horse breeder had met Penelope had changed everything for them all.

Yes, his curiosity was a good thing, and Annie Cahill made him curious and he longed to unravel the mystery that surrounded her. Why should a woman with a good position wish to leave it and take the chance on a stranger? Why did her plain and simple words make him feel as if he had known her for a lifetime? Why did he want to find out more about her? He let Penelope leave the room and began to pen a reply, there was so much he simply had to know and he had a feeling that just a correspondence spread over weeks and months as their missives crossed the entire breadth of the country wasn't going to be enough to unravel the mystery she posed to him quickly enough.

# Chapter Three

The letter that sat on Annie's bed was much thicker than anything she had ever received before. She didn't often receive mail, and rarely on such fine paper. The envelope was creamy, and the parchment like paper was soft and silky under her fingertips. She opened it carefully, keen not to damage even the tiniest bit of such elegant stationery. She pulled out quite a short letter and a train ticket to Great Falls, Montana. She picked it up and looked it over. She was sure it must be some kind of prank, or mistake. She only knew one person in Montana, and Myra's handwriting was altogether neater and prettier. Then she remembered, she had answered that ridiculous advertisement. It had been weeks, and it truly had slipped her mind as she had been so very busy.

He had responded, and had sent a ticket for her to use to join him. If it weren't so preposterous she could have jumped for joy. Who sent a ticket to a woman he had barely corresponded with? She should be ashamed of herself for presuming it meant he intended marriage immediately too – for her heart had definitely leapt with excitement at the prospect – because a one way ticket could only mean one thing, surely?

*Dear Miss Cahill,*

*Thank you for your response to my advertisement. I am in good health I am gratified to let you know. Your hasty and apparently uncharacteristic missive pleased me and left me with many questions I simply must have answered. But, I must first do you the courtesy of enquiring after your wellbeing and pray that this finds you in the very best of health.*

*Please forgive my presumption for including a ticket at this ridiculously early stage of our correspondence, but I understand you are acquainted with the wife of one of my closest friends, Carlton Green. Dear Myra has offered to have you come for a short visit, so that we may see if we might suit. I do hope you will not mind my having spoken to them before I asked you – but when my sister Penelope put two and two together from the information in your letter I couldn't contain my curiosity that there may be somebody acquainted to you living just across the valley!*

*Please, if it is possible for you to do such a thing, I ask you humbly to join us here in Sun River for a short visit. It is a truly wonderful corner of the world. There are craggy, snow-capped mountains surrounding us and the valley is rich and fertile. Should you wish to, I would love to be able to show you the beautiful features of my home – especially the waterfalls that give the nearby town of Great Falls its name – there are five, and all spectacular in their own way. Sun River is a tiny hamlet, with only a few basic shops and a Saloon, but it is growing fast and looks likely to blossom in time. There is a good community, and the local minister comes to visit us every Sunday for services if you wished to attend.*

*There are three of us that farm here. Carlton grows crops; my sister Penelope's fiancé, Callum Walters, breeds fine horses and I raise cattle. So, we ride on sturdy mounts, eat well-grown grains and vegetables and have plenty of good quality beef – reasons to visit a place if ever there were any I hope. But the true blessings of this place are the people who live here and work here. It is an industrious community, and people have little free time – but they care greatly about each other and are always willing to lend a hand if they can. I hope that you will like it, at least as much as Mrs Green seems to be doing. She is settling in and making friends well, I am sure you will be glad to know.*

*Now, I believe you wanted to know a little bit about me. I am a bit of a lone wolf by nature. I enjoy ranching because it means I get to spend so much time alone, in the wild. I grew up in New York, always felt it too claustrophobic. There seemed to be so few opportunities. I was expected to become a ship builder like my Father, yet I could not take to that life. I became a sailor for a short time, travelled the world but never saw more than the ports of anyplace I travelled too. Soon I felt just as stifled being aboard a tiny boat as I had trapped in the city.*

*So, I came home and found that in my absence my Father had sadly passed away. Mama and Penelope were living on the tiny amounts I managed to send home. Something had to change, and so when the newspapers started talking about land, for free if you could work it and make it pay I tried to convince them that this was our chance. Penelope was all for it, but Mama didn't want to leave her home and friends. I could understand that, and so I tried to find work in the city as a laborer. There is always work in the docks, and so I spent my days as a stevedore, my nights I am ashamed to say were spent in bars. I tried to drink away my unhappiness.*

*Eventually I could take it no more, and I said that I was coming here, to Montana, whether my family would accompany me or not. I truly believe that I might not be still here had I not done so. Penelope would have followed me anywhere, but Mama did not wish to leave still. However, my Aunt Gwen was glad to take her in as my Uncle Harold had passed away and she too was lonely. They are both now thriving. They do all manner of charity work around the tenements near the docks. So many people have so very little there and disease is rife. They do good work and are content.*

*I have not been back to New York in over seven years, but I should like to see Mama. Penelope hopes she will come to Montana for her wedding, but I am not so sure she would be up to the journey. Even with the convenience of the station at Great Falls the journey is long and can be very draining (that possibly isn't what you long to hear as I try to convince you to come!) I should love to have the time to undertake the journey to see her – but cattle need care at all times. This is why I have included the ticket for you. Much as I would like to be able to meet you in Boston it simply isn't possible for me to do so.*

*I do enjoy reading, though I rarely get time to finish an entire novel, so I enjoy the short stories they sometimes publish in the newspapers, and poetry. I am writing this having just seen a rather splendid play in the theatre at Great Falls, and I quite like music – though I have never been much for opera. But I am happiest when I am out on horseback, riding across this majestic land, enjoying the sun on my skin and wind in my hair.*

*Your letter, though short gave me so many questions I long to ask of you. I want to know if you have ever been anywhere other than Boston; have you any family; what truly makes your heart beat faster and makes you feel alive are just a few of the many things I long to know about you. You gave so little away – and I have to say for an inquisitive soul like myself that was too much to resist.*

*I do not want a wife to just take care of house and hearth, though my love of the land and being free may indeed sound that way. I long for a wife who will be a true helpmeet, a partner and, if I may be so bold, a lover. This is why I believe it so important that we meet, and soon to find out if such things could ever be possible for us and so I can begin to unravel the enigma that you pose my dear!*

*I look forward to your response, and pray that I shall be able to meet you at the station should you accept my invitation to Montana.*

*Yours Hopefully*
*Mackenzie Stott*

Annie sighed and clasped the letter to her breast. He made it all sound so wonderfully easy. But though he was able to comprehend that a trip to Boston to visit with her would be impossible given his commitments in Montana, he did not seem to appreciate that should she request the time needed for such a stay that she would most surely lose her position here. It was a huge gamble to take, one she was not sure she was quite ready to take on such a short correspondence.

His letter had amused her, and his outpourings had made her realize what a passionate and exciting man he must be, and also so unlike his advertisement in truth. He would be more than disappointed when he met her she was sure; she was such a mouse after all. There was little interesting about her. She had never been outside of a three block radius, let alone travelled the high seas and traipsed across the country in search of adventure as he had. Reluctantly she put the letter down and accepted that the simple and straightforward man she had so longed for did not exist – and that she would have to write to him later to end their correspondence. It was not fair to him, or to herself to continue to live in a fantasy world. She could not lie to him, make out that she was more than she truly was. She would not set herself up for such potential heartache.

The next days passed in their usual drudgery, yet the sunshine seemed to beckon to her, coaxing her out to play and explore. Each day she tried to find the time to go for a solitary walk, to feel the wind and the warmth on her skin the way Mackenzie had written of it. She had never stopped to notice such things before, had never taken the time to really appreciate what was around her every day. Now it seemed his words echoed in her head, and she felt more, saw more, and heard more than she ever had until now. The birds in the trees, the chatter and giggle of children playing in the park, and the pleasure of lifting her face up towards the sun. It felt wonderful, as if there was an entire world that she didn't even know about, and the more she did it the more she knew she had to do so again and again.

She still hadn't replied to him, and knew that it might be that her letter may not now reach him until after the date her train should be arriving. She wasn't sure what had stayed her hand. She had been so certain that she could not take such an indulgent risk, yet here she was feeling nervous and agitated. She wasn't unhappy, not exactly, just discontented. It was as if she had been walking round with scales over her eyes obscuring her view, and that Mackenzie's words had sloughed them away, letting her see the world clearly for the very first time. It was interesting, and vast, and she found herself longing to see something more than the inside of another family's home, though that little voice in the back of her head wouldn't stop telling her that she didn't deserve such pleasure, such joy, such hope.

"Annie, the new governess will be arriving tomorrow. I trust you will ensure her room is aired and cleaned meticulously. I do not want her to get the wrong impression of us," Mrs Hepworth said haughtily from the end of the corridor as Annie was just taking off her coat and boots. She felt her little moment of bliss slip away from her as the demands of reality took over once more. "I shan't ask where you have been when you should have been here working. I have been calling for you for a quarter of an hour, and that simply isn't good enough. Really, I don't know what has gotten into you in the past few days."

Annie knew better than to respond, to argue or even to try and explain anything. Mrs Hepworth didn't care about anything other than putting on a show to the rest of the world. The pretentiousness of the entire house and the extravagant parties they threw just made it more obvious to anyone who had ever been around those from the genuine upper classes. Annie's first position had been in the Boston home of an English Earl. The house had been filled with old family treasures, most ugly but all worth more than the entire contents of the Hepworth house. He hadn't cared one jot what anyone thought of him, or his home. He hadn't needed to. His title had bought him access to every drawing room and ballroom in the city without any effort. She missed working in such a place, but she couldn't bear to think about why she had been forced to leave.

Mrs Hepworth was still standing in the service corridor, looking down her long nose disdainfully at her. Annie suddenly felt the mischievous and adventurous spirit that seemed to have overtaken her in recent days begin to exert itself. Unable, and even unusually unwilling, to keep it under control she decided to stand up for herself, just this once. "Ma'am, all of my chores were completed and so I took a walk. The park is quite lovely with all the flowers coming into bloom." Mrs Hepworth sniffed and the furrows between her eyebrows deepened as she frowned down at Annie.

"Your chores are complete only when nobody in this house has no further need of you. It is not for you to decide when you may take time away from your duties." Annie looked at her incredulously. She knew her place, did not need to be told. She had never so much as considered breaking a single rule in the five years she had been in this household. Yet, she could not remember a single time when this woman had ever complimented her on a job well done. The strong and determined young woman she had spent so long trying to damp down and keep under wraps decided to take control. Annie was going to do something for herself, something that would make her happy. Suddenly she was certain that the consequences were more than worth it.

"Ma'am, I am glad you have sought me out as I have needed to speak with you," she said hurriedly as Mrs Hepworth made to move away, clearly she believed that there was nothing further that needed to be addressed. But for once Annie was not going to bite her tongue, was not going to be so careful that she actually ran away from life.

"Annie, I have better things to do," her employer said impatiently turning on her heel. It clearly wasn't the best time to be broaching this, but for the first time in her life Annie felt reckless. It didn't matter what happened. She knew Myra would not let her be homeless, would help her to find a position either back here in Boston, or in Montana if she needed one, should things with Mackenzie not work out. She was still young enough to have a life of her own. She was not going to stay and take any more from this cold and unfeeling woman.

"I wanted to let you know I need to take a leave of absence. I will need to be away for at least two months."

"Is your Mother sick?"

"No. My Mother died three years ago. You attended her funeral."

"Then what possible reason could you have to need such a period of time?" Mrs Hepworth said, undaunted by Annie's words. "I cannot spare you for even a day right now. The new governess is coming and will need your assistance in settling in and we have Carolynn's coming out ball to arrange after all. No, you simply cannot take the time right now."

"Then I shall have to offer you my notice."

"Don't be so ridiculous girl. What would possess you to be so foolhardy?"

"I am going to meet the man I hope to marry, not that it is any of your business. I have a life separate from my work Ma'am, and if you will not release me from my contract and offer me a character, then I shall go without one and have to take my chances." Mrs Hepworth's face told Annie that for once, she had managed to finally penetrate this woman's cold façade, and had shaken her to the core.

"But Caro's ball? Mr Hepworth will be furious!"

"And I am afraid that shall be your problem to deal with and not mine Ma'am. I shall be catching a train on Monday, so if you could possibly ensure that my wages are ready at the end of the week?"

"Your impertinence is noted, and there shall be no character, you little slut. How dare you do this to me? I shall not ensure your wages are ready, you have given me no notice and will leave me in a position that is simply untenable." Mrs Hepworth's handsome face was screwed up with venomous anger, but rather than feeling cowed, Annie actually felt vindicated.

"Ma'am. I have been doing my own work and that of the governess for two months, I am sure that the new governess can do the same," she said cheekily. "And, I shall go and see the gentleman that so ably assisted Mr Green with his little matter if you insist on not paying me. I am sure that a judge would perceive your not paying me what I am owed as being most inappropriate." Mrs Hepworth didn't seem to know what to say to that, she made an odd noise, something between a harrumph and a snort, and Annie had to hold back her giggles. "Oh, I was going to suggest a couple of young women who may have been available to assist you in my absence had you agreed to it, but I am inclined now to just let you find your own new maid. I wouldn't recommend working here to a single soul now."

Before she could lose her nerve Annie ran upstairs to her room. She had never been so rude, had never stood up for herself and her own wants and it felt peculiar. She felt equal parts of elation, fear, excitement and guilt. But she had paved the way for a new life. She could only hope that Mackenzie would not find her too dull and boring when he met her and realized this truly was the most dangerous and undoubtedly the most foolish risk she had ever taken.

# Chapter Four

The herd veered left at speed. Mack cursed under his breath, and wheeled his horse around to try and corral them into the pen before they stampeded through the yard and straight through his house. He hated to admit it, but he really needed to get some help now the numbers of cattle had grown so large. It wouldn't take much for him to be the unsuspecting victim of a panicked charge. He vowed to see if there were any cowboys hanging around the saloon the next time he was in Sun River. If he had some help then he could leave these dawn starts to them, he certainly wouldn't miss them one bit. "Whoah there girls and boys," he hollered as he managed to outflank them and shoo the bolting steers and cows back towards the holding pen.

As he dismounted and fixed the gate he looked up at the sky. A grey cloud had been looming, and he was pretty sure that the heavens would open long before he had them sorted. He needed to separate out the pregnant cows from the herd to make sure they were healthy and everything was progressing as it should for them and to mark up any expecting twins. They would need extra care, and he would keep them in the paddocks close to the farm so he could bring them into the barn easily when their time to calve came. The steers would need to go back up into the foothills to fatten up before the thankfully short drive across country to Great Falls and then on by train to every State in the Union.

"Mack, Mack, where are you?" his sister called loudly. He could hear a note of panic in her voice. "Mack, you have to get to Great Falls!"

"Penny, you aren't making any sense. I've nothing to do but sort out this mangy lot," he said as he ruffled the soft brown head of one of his pregnant cows who was nosily poking her head over the gate, his stomach growling the need for breakfast.

"There's a letter. It's from her. I'm sorry, I opened it by mistake, but she is coming. She will be on the train today!" She thrust the envelope at him and he took it and looked from it and then back to her.

"But, if she is coming why didn't she let me know before? I thought she wasn't coming," he repeated foolishly. Penelope laid a soothing hand on his arm, hearing the way his voice had cracked. He truly had given up hope of hearing from her. He had convinced himself that he must have come on too strongly, or expected more of her than she was able to give and so she had simply decided to end their correspondence. It had felt strange to him. Even though they had only shared a few letters he felt he knew her, and she didn't seem to be the kind of person who would do that. But it had been easier to bear that way, because he had already begun to anticipate when another letter would come. He had been downcast when nothing had arrived day after day.

He took out the letter and read the few short lines Annie had penned, clearly in haste.

> *Dear Mackenzie (I hope you do not think me too forward using your Christian name, I rather like it. It is a little raffish and mysterious!)*
>
> *I am on my way to Montana. I am so very sorry I did not write sooner – but I wasn't going to come. I thought I would lose my position if I asked to for the time needed to travel for an extended stay (and I was right, I have managed exactly that!). I wasn't sure I was ready to take the chance on so short an acquaintance. I was*

*scared I would give up everything only to arrive in Sun River and to have you dislike me. You said you want a true helpmeet, a lover and not just a wife. I wasn't sure I could deliver that. You sounded so very full of life, and courage. I have none. I have done nothing in my life and am so terribly dull. But I found that I have a devilish little imp inside me that has awakened. She wants to take some risks, and so I am coming. I shall be with you very soon. I can only pray you will not be disappointed in me.*

*Yours in all hopefulness*
*Annie Cahill*

"I'd better get to town!" Mack gasped as his heart soared. She was coming, and she had risked everything to do so – for him. He knew it was too soon to know, but he prayed that she would find him amiable, that she would be the gentle calming soul her letters seemed to convey to him. But he was also more than pleased to find that she too had a reckless side, and could take risks when she felt it right. She trusted herself, as he trusted himself and he could only hope they would learn to trust one another.

"I think she must like you too," Penelope said sagely. "No woman would take such a chance on a complete stranger if she didn't. Be careful, don't you hurt her."

"I see you already care more for her than you do me – what if she hurts me? You didn't think of that possibility did you?" His sister merely smiled at him, turned and walked away without comment. "Penny, please can you ride over to Carlton's place and tell him he's got a visitor on the way?"

"Why should I?"

"For Annie, not me. It will be strange enough just coming out here and she will be exhausted from the journey. It wasn't so long ago that we came out here, remember how tough it was? The least we can do on her first night in Montana is to ensure there is a friendly face that she recognizes watching over her."

"You didn't need to beg! I'm on my way right now," she said infuriatingly and marched back towards him and untethered Blackie from the fence. In moments she was up on his back and racing across the fields to the Green farm. He couldn't deny it; she truly was an incredible horsewoman. He should have gotten her out with the herds rather than letting her keep house for him – she could outride and out jump him any day of the week.

Mack rushed across the yard, and lowered the bucket down into the well. He didn't have the time to have a real bath, he would already be late, most likely, but he was determined that he wouldn't smell too badly of horse and cattle when he met her. He wanted to make a good impression, not have her racing to get straight back on the train. He made his way over to the stable and pulled out the gig. It was covered in dust, it so rarely got used. He quickly ran an old cloth over it, removing the worst of the filth but it still looked terrible. He had no choice though, it was this or nothing. Carefully he pulled out the harness from the back seat, and prayed it would last the journey. It was worn in too many places, but Penny's old mare, Mildred, was docile enough and wouldn't strain between the shafts too much so they should be fine.

In just ten minutes he was on the road, and on his way into Great Falls. As he drove he kept on thinking about Annie and what she had given up to be here, to be with him. To think he might have not known, and that she could have been stranded in a place where she knew no-one. He shook his head, and clicked to Mildred to go just a little faster. He didn't want to push her too hard, the roads were a little rutted after the heavy rains and then baking sunshine they had seen recently. But the old girl took it well and they made good time, reaching Great Falls just after lunchtime.

The train was due at twenty five minutes past two o'clock. He glanced up at the big station clock and saw he still had twenty minutes. He rushed to the bakery on the main street and bought himself a meat pie and some dainty pastries for them both for the journey home. He devoured his pie whilst walking back to the station at pace. He wanted to be there waiting for her. He certainly didn't want her to think that he didn't care for her enough to be there to meet her. He paced up and down nervously, now wishing he hadn't bolted his repast so quickly – it had only given the butterflies in his belly fuel and they were making the most of it.

Finally he saw the clouds of smoke and steam coming around the bend and heard the whistle of the train. He watched avidly as the great iron beast pulled up. He was fascinated by the lumbering great machines. Their huge power and their ability to take you almost anywhere you wanted to go appealed to him greatly. He wondered if he would ever get the chance to go in search of adventure ever again. The ranch needed him now, but maybe one day he would be able to go in search of new experiences. He wondered if Annie would be keen to join him, or if her one experience of travel would be enough for her.

He suddenly realized that he knew nothing of what Annie looked like. How would he ever recognize her? Was she petite, blonde, a redhead? He had no clue, and as the smoke billowed around him he wondered if he would ever be able to find her anyway. He could barely see his own hand in front of his face. But as the smoke finally cleared he saw a small woman standing nervously a few yards ahead of him, biting her lip and clasping and re-clasping her hands. She had delicate features, a smattering of freckles across the bridge of her tiny, tilted nose, and a figure with curves any man would be glad to explore. She wore a smart blue hat that matched her coat exactly and clean white gloves on her small hands.

Mack was rarely lost for words, but seeing her standing there and looking so lost and vulnerable he was speechless. He felt his breath catch in his chest as he moved towards her, and he longed to hold her and reassure her that everything would be fine, that he would take care of her, that she had nothing to fear. Yet the words would not come, he stood gaping at her, sure his mouth was wide open like a cod fish.

"Mr Mackenzie Stott?" she asked him after some time had passed. He jolted.

"Sorry, yes, yes. Annie Cahill I presume?" he said trying desperately to cover up his embarrassment at being stuck for words at the very sight of her. "How was your journey? I only received your letter this morning – I very nearly wasn't here to greet you!"

"I am so very sorry, it was such a spur of the moment decision. I so very nearly didn't come. I was so fearful of what I would lose; I simply couldn't focus on the things I might gain." Mack was aware how quickly they were both speaking, how breathless they both were and laughed. "I'm sorry," Annie asked with a quizzical look, "did I say something funny?"

"No, I was struck by how we are both so very nervous that we are speaking so rapidly to cover it up," he said. Her expression softened a little. "I am sorry, this isn't going the way I planned it. Can we maybe start again?"

# Chapter Five

Annie looked at his face. It was a kind face, but rugged and tanned from his work out on the land. His eyes were the most vivid hazel she had ever seen and she could barely tear her eyes from them to even take into consideration the rest of him. He was very tall, she had to crane her neck to look up to him, but the fine features and laughing eyes made it worth any ounce of pain. Reluctantly she tore her eyes away from his, and looked him over quickly. She didn't wish to appear rude, and so she made her passing glimpse swift. She took in his broad shoulders and the tapering hips that made her feel tiny and powerless. It was an odd sensation, she had never really thought of herself as being particularly weak, or even that feminine before, but he made her feel as delicate as a china doll. He truly was an impressive figure of manhood, and she would have had to have been half dead to not find him attractive – but that just made her even more nervous.

"Of course," she said, finally responding to his gently asked question. "It is a pleasure to meet you Mr Stott." Awkwardly she looked down towards her feet and held out her hand for him to shake. He clasped it and held it tenderly for a moment. She couldn't help but notice his large, strong hands with those long and tapering fingers. She could see tiny scars where he had suffered nicks and cuts as he undertook his work, and feel the hard skin from riding out on the land and pulling on ropes on board ships. They were hands that would always catch you if you fell, she thought as a bolt of electricity flashed through her entire body.

"The pleasure is all mine," he said, his deep baritone voice rippling through her like music. He bent down and raised her hand to his lips and, in a move she hadn't expected, turned the palm over and unfastened her glove. He pressed his lips slowly to the inside of her wrist, and then carefully buttoned her back up. Her entire body quivered. Nobody had ever done such a thing to her before; it was so intimate, so sensual. Whatever she might think of him as a man, her body was certainly more than happy to respond to his advances. She felt light, shivery, almost faint with pleasure as he took her arm and tucked it into his own.

"So, how was your journey?" he asked politely again.

"It was an experience," she admitted with a wry smile. She had never been so frightened in her life. "There was a gentleman in my carriage; he didn't say a word to a soul the entire journey. We were all sure he was some kind of gangster, or gun for hire. He certainly didn't seem the warm and friendly type. He had the most spectacular moustache, and was constantly chewing on a small piece of wood – and he stared at everyone as if he hated us all."

"He sounds horrible, but it sounds as if you managed to make some friends to at the very least discuss his peccadilloes with?"

"I did. There was a lovely older couple, they got off at Billings, were going to see their daughter. She married a banker apparently and is expecting. And then there was Mr Craven. He is a Minister, is going to be building a chapel somewhere near us I believe. They were all most kind." He stopped her by an old gig. It was sturdy, but clearly hadn't been used in some time."I can only apologize for the gig my dear, as I said I only got word first thing this morning that you were coming and so it is a little dirty," Mackenzie said, as if he was reading her mind. She looked up at him, a smile on her face.

"I don't mind dirt. I've been a maid for over ten years Mr Stott, dirt I can handle in spades," she said bravely. She was rewarded with a huge grin. He had the cutest dimples and his eyes literally sparkled when he was happy. She let him assist her onto the dashboard of the gig, and watched as he heaved her trunk up behind her. He barely seemed to have to even step into the tiny carriage, his legs were so long, and it looked a little uncomfortable for him to be so cramped up as he clicked to the horse to get moving.

She didn't really know what to say to him, and suddenly she felt utterly exhausted. He smiled down at her. "You look about all in," he said as he pulled a blanket from under the seat and tucked it around her knees. "I know it's warm now, but as the sun starts to set it will get quite chilly – and if you are tired you'll probably need to sleep. Don't you worry if that pretty little head of yours nods its way over to lean on my shoulder, I'll take good care of you and have you safely tucked up with Myra in no time at all." Gratefully she tucked herself up against him, and as the waves of tiredness engulfed her she soon drifted into a light sleep. She hadn't felt so safe since she had left home all those years ago and she allowed herself to sink deeper into her dreams.

"Miss Cahill, Annie wake up! Are you alright? You were screaming and moaning," Mackenzie said, his face a picture of concern as she was jolted awake. She gazed around at the huge mountains and the unfamiliar scenery, but was completely disorientated by the feel of his big, warm hands on her own. It was entirely too delicious, and distracting and she pulled away quickly.

"Oh, I was only dreaming," she said dismissively. She wasn't ready to admit those dreams to anybody, certainly not a man she barely knew. She had never spoken of the reason why she had left the Earl's employ, and she wasn't ready to face up to it and speak of it now – or ever. But it was good that he cared for her, though she was left wondering why she should have the nightmare now, of all times. She hadn't had the dreams in years though they had once been a part of her everyday existence, torturing her and making her dread the nighttime hours. No, it was just because she was overtired, and that everything was so strange and new. She was bound to feel a little discombobulated, she would get over it all in no time, and she would never need to speak of it ever again.

"We can go on now, I'd like to rest properly and I can't wait to see Myra and Carlton again," she said determined to change the subject, though something in Mackenzie's eyes told her that he may let her off now because she was tired, but that he wasn't the kind of man to let such a thing go entirely. She would need to remember that, and to make sure he never suspected that it was anything more than just a bad dream because she was so utterly and completely fatigued.

"Well, if you are sure, but I'm here if you ever want to tell me anything. I am like a closed book – I never tell anyone's secrets to a soul," he assured her. "Now you're awake I can tell you a little bit about Montana as we go if you'd like?"

"That would be lovely," Annie said glad of the change of subject and the chance to bury her thoughts and fears where they belonged once more. "Can you tell me about the mountains please? They truly are majestic, aren't they?"

Annie barely heard a word Mackenzie said, but he seemed happy enough to give her the full guided tour of his home. She sat quietly and wondered why she had ever thought that this could be a good idea. She should have known that those memories would come back at some point. She couldn't bear it. She simply didn't know what to do. Mackenzie was such a nice man and he genuinely seemed to care for her. She couldn't drag him into her own personal hell; it would not be fair on him. Yet, she so desperately wanted to be free of it all, to be able to start a new life. Why should such a thing, one not of her doing, have the potential to ruin everything?

# Chapter Six

Mack rushed through the sorting, he simply couldn't wait to be finished so he could ride over to Carlton's place and see Annie once more. She was such a petite and pretty little thing, and despite being so tired she had shown a real interest and appreciation for the landscape they had driven through the day before. He wanted her to meet Penelope, and to see his home and the ranch, to meet his cattle and see everything. But he had a feeling that he may need to take things slowly. The nightmare she had endured told him she was more fragile than she wanted him to believe her to be. There was something in her past she had buried, and he had to find a way to help her to move past it.

He had seen many men, mainly in his days at sea, that had allowed old memories to fester and to congeal around their hearts. It made them unable to trust another soul and left them lonely and unhappy. He would not wish such a bitter existence on anyone, much less on the woman he was determined he would make his wife. He had never felt such a pull towards another soul before. Something in her called to something in him and he felt powerless to resist it. She thought she was dull, and of no consequence – but he saw something so very different. She was feisty and full of courage. She was honest and caring. He didn't know why or how, but she had captured his heart right from her very first letter.

"I brought you your breakfast, I presume you will be tearing off across the valley as soon as you are done," Penelope said with a twinkle in her eye.

"Would you like to come with me?" Mack asked, knowing his sister well enough to know that she would be itching to meet Annie as soon as possible.

"I'll let you have her to yourself today brother, but I shall invite her to supper tomorrow. Maybe we could invite Myra and Carlton too?"

"That sounds like a wonderful idea and thank you for my breakfast." He bit down into the large hunk of freshly baked bread, and then took a bite of the cheese she had handed to him in a bright red kerchief. He munched contentedly, and looked out over the land. He truly loved his home. He could only hope that Annie would fall in love with it, even if she couldn't fall in love with him – at least that way she would stay.

His breakfast consumed, he saddled Blackie and Mildred and put her on a lead rein, then set out. The sun was peeking in and out of fluffy clouds, but a large storm cloud was hovering off to the East. He wondered if it would hit today or later that evening. The wind was light, barely a gentle breeze. Maybe they would be lucky and he would be able to take Annie to see the Falls? He was sure she would find them breathtaking, and he couldn't think of a more romantic spot to ask her to be his wife. He knew it was sudden, probably too sudden, but he knew he didn't want to wait – knew that she was the only woman he wanted to spend his life with. So, why wait?

"Good morning neighbor," Carlton drawled with a huge grin on his handsome face. "I was expecting you at the crack of dawn!"

"I had cattle to sort – got interrupted yesterday, otherwise I might have been here even before the sun came up," Mack joked.

"She's a pretty little thing. Myra and she have been giggling and gossiping all morning – but she works!"

"What do you mean?" Mack thundered, Annie was supposed to be a guest in their home, not unpaid labor.

"Hold your horses, she was up before us both and had the kitchen spotless before we even knew what she was at. Said she wanted to be busy. I think she's a bit nervous. Be gentle with her." Mack stared at his boots, what if she was nervous because she didn't like him? What if she had realized she had made a terrible mistake in coming here, and keeping busy was the only way to stop herself from thinking of it?

"What have I done?" he said, taking off his Stetson and running his fingers through his hair.

"Stop that right now," Carlton said. "She's fine. Tiredness can do funny things to a woman. Myra was up all through her first night too; fidgeting and moving things around. It takes people a while to settle to anything new."

"Of course, you are right. I can't expect her to just fit, to know that this is right."

"But you do?" Carlton asked curiously.

"I do. I knew from her first letter."

"Me too, with Myra. Though she was the only letter I got - unlike you! I feel for you my friend. It is hard when we fall –especially until the day you are sure they have too."

Their conversation was stopped as Myra appeared out on the porch. "Well good morning Mackenzie. I presume you would like to take Annie out today? Do you need me to come along as a chaperone?" she teased as she gave him a welcoming peck on the cheek.

"I don't know, do you think it would make her feel more at ease?" Mack said anxiously.

"I think you will be fine. She is a sensible woman, knows her own mind. I'll just go and get her."

Mack paced up and down on the creaking deck, he hadn't ever though that something so simple as taking a girl for a picnic could ever make him so nervous, but his stomach was churning. "Ow," he exclaimed, as he bit too deep at the skin around his finger nails – a habit he had thought he had long ago abandoned.

"Good morning Mr Stott," Annie said in her sweet voice as she came through the screen door. She was wearing a pretty floral dress and her hair was lying in rippling waves down her back. He longed to bury his hands in the silky tresses and pull her to him for a kiss. But, the amused looks of his friends stopped him.

"I think it's time you called me Mackenzie, or Mack," he replied. "May I call you Annie?" She grinned, and he smiled back at her. "So, would you like to go for a ride?"

"But, I don't know how."

"I can teach you. I brought Mildred, she's old and steady. Penelope learned to ride on her when we first moved here and she's a better rider than anyone I know now. Mildred will teach you in no time." She nodded, but he could see a touch of wariness in her eyes still.

"I shall pack you both a good lunch," Myra said generously.

"No need, I have a saddle bag full of goodies, and an invitation for you all to join us for supper tomorrow from Penny. Do say you will all come?"

"We would be delighted," Carlton said as he moved to stand beside his wife and put an arm around her waist. Mack couldn't help but wish that he could do the same to Annie, to simply take her in his arms and reassure her that he would never let any harm come to her. But instead he stood awkwardly and said nothing.

"Shall we go then?" Annie finally said as she moved towards him. She took his hand and began to lead him down the steps towards the horses. "Now, how on earth do I get up there?" He put his hands around her waist and carefully lifted her into place.

"I hope you don't mind riding astride, we don't have a side saddle and very few women out here ride that way. Maybe we could get you some breeches if you decide you like it – that is what Penny wears."

"You are babbling again," Annie teased.

"I can't help it," he whispered so only she could hear. "You make me nervous."

"I cannot think why. I am not the scary type," she confided in him, leaning down to whisper in his ear. The gentle touch of her breath against the sensitive skin of his neck made him shiver.

"Oh, I think you are far scarier than you could ever imagine." She laughed and watched him closely as he mounted. He had never felt so exposed, so anxious to please anyone. He gently squeezed his heels into Blackie's side, and keeping a tight hold on Mildred's lead rein they walked slowly out of the yard and up onto one of the gently worn trails.

"I'll keep you on the rein until you feel a little more confident," he said as he dismounted once they reached a beautiful meadow full of wild flowers. "Would you like to trot? You'll need to stand up a little in the stirrups as you do, rise and fall with the movement otherwise your backside will be sore as anything!"

"Why not?" she said, her pretty face lighting up with her determination. Carefully he showed her how to squeeze just so into Mildred's flanks so the old horse would pick up her speed just a little, and watched carefully as she began to bounce around in the saddle a little. "I don't think I've quite got it!"

"Just feel the rhythm, and then rise and fall along with it," he encouraged her as Mildred turned in a wide circle around him.

On her third go she got the movement just right and her face was alight with joy. He grinned idiotically at her, as proud as she was of her achievements. "Want to go a little faster?" he said with a mischievous chuckle.

"Uh-huh," she said and carefully did as he told her to bring Mildred to a gentle canter. On her fourth circle he let go of the lead rein, and Annie didn't even notice that she was riding alone.

"Now, squeeze her again and go a little faster," he encouraged her. Mildred responded and moved into a sedate gallop, She was too old now for much more, but Mack could see how much Annie was enjoying herself. "Now pull back on the reins very gently and sit back in the saddle and she will naturally come to a gentle halt." Annie's face was a picture when she did exactly what she had been told and the well schooled old mare did exactly as she was asked.

"I rode!" she exclaimed happily.

"You did indeed. And very well too. You have lovely light hands, you'll not hurt her mouth and you learn very quickly," he said admiringly. She suddenly flipped her weight, bringing her leg over and dismounted just as he had done, landing right in front of him, so close he could feel the heat coming from her body. "Really fast," he said with an appreciative whistle.

"This is wonderful. Will I get to ride a lot if I stay here?"

"You can ride all day every day if you want to. You can come out with me with the herds, we can get you your own gun and a neat little holster to put it in," he teased as he mapped out where it would lie against her hip with his hands.

"I'd like that," she said breathlessly. Unable to stop himself, he dipped his head and kissed her rosy lips. They tasted sweet, and he pulled her to him as she began to respond tentatively. Her fingers crept up and began to twine around the curls at his nape, and he allowed himself to bury his hands in her long blonde locks. Breaking away he gazed into her eyes tenderly.

"Annie, I know we barely know one another, but will you marry me?" he asked her, knowing his hopes and dreams were written all over his face – she merely had to look at him to see how she set him on fire.

She pulled away abruptly. He looked at her, confused. She had been right there with him. That kiss had been mutual, and he was sure she cared for him too. Her face had gone cold, closed – as it had been when he had questioned her about her dream the day before. "I'm sorry. I should never have come, should never have thought that I could do this," she spluttered as she tried to move further from him, but Mildred's sturdy body was in her way. "Please," she begged, then turned to bury her face in the horse's body to hide the tears that had begun to fall. Mack spun her to face him.

"No! Now, you are going to tell me what this is all about. You clammed up on me yesterday, and I will not let you fob me off again."

"It is nothing. I can't change it. You can't change it. So what difference would it make?"

"It is clearly making a difference, if you cannot even tell me what the matter is. I may not be able to change it – but I can hopefully put your mind at rest and let you know that it doesn't matter. Nothing could be so very bad that you cannot even tell me."

"If I tell you, you will send me straight back to Boston and there is nothing for me there. You will never look at me like that again, and you will certainly never want me to be your wife."

# Chapter Seven

Mack stared at her, but his face was not angry –just terribly sad. She longed to reach up and kiss the little lines around his eyes and on his forehead until they softened and went away, but it was not her right. She should never have come here. She should have known that her past would catch up to her, that she would never be free of it. Mackenzie was a good, kind man and he deserved a good wife, a chaste wife, an honest wife. But she could not bring herself to admit to her deepest and darkest secrets to him, or anyone.

"Annie, I am waiting," he said firmly. "Whatever you think is so bad that you could never be my wife cannot be as bad as you think. Your past is your past. I am far more interested in your future – your future here with me." Annie so longed to believe his words, but he was making promises he couldn't keep. No man could. How could any man ever accept her as she was, as soiled goods?

"Mr Stott, please do not make this harder on us both. I shall get the first train back as soon as I can. You will forget about me in no time and will find yourself a wife worthy of the name."

"I think you are worthy of the name of Mrs Stott and I have yet to learn anything that tells me otherwise Annie – and my name is Mackenzie."

"Stop this, please. I just can't," she cried tearing away from him and running as fast as she could. She had no clue where she was going, but she just couldn't be so close to him and keep her wits. Everything about him overwhelmed her, and she longed to give in – to believe he truly could forgive her anything but she knew that men simply couldn't do that. Society couldn't do that.

"Annie," she heard his heavy footfalls behind her. "ANNIE!" She turned, he had tears pouring down his cheeks too. Without thinking she reached up to wipe them away. He held her palm against his face and just gazed into her eyes. "I love you. Whatever you have done, I am certain that I have probably done worse. If you will tell me of your demons I shall gladly tell you of mine." Mesmerized by the sincerity in his hazel eyes she nodded and then sank to her knees in the long grass. He collapsed beside her and took her hand firmly in his. He took a deep breath and then began to speak softly.

"When I was at sea, I was lonely. I was never anywhere for very long and so like many sailors I often used to go to the brothels. We would get drunk and sometimes the women were badly used. Not by me, but I did nothing to stop my shipmates from doing so. For a brief while I served onboard a pirate ship, and we did some unspeakable things – but it meant I could send money home to my family to keep them safe. Nobody is perfect Annie, and I doubt if you have killed just so you can take the cargo from another man's ship, or ever used another human being ill, or stood by while such a thing was done. You are too good and too kind."

Annie stared at him; his confession was not what she had expected of him. She had guessed from his last letter that he had a past that was possibly more colorful than anyone she had ever known, but to think she was sat beside a real life pirate was strangely exciting. She simply couldn't reconcile the sweet and gentle man who sat by her side now with her idea of a cut-throat privateer.

"I don't believe you."

"You don't have to." He pulled up his sleeve and showed her a brand on his arm. "It is the mark they give you in the Indies if you are caught as the member of a pirate crew. I was lucky I wasn't hanged – but the Governor benefited from an unexpected cargo of rum – enough to keep him soused for many years - and our lives were spared." Annie giggled nervously. It was her turn, and though she knew he would not be as understanding of her past, she had to let him know that it didn't matter to her what he had done.

"You would never do such a thing again?"

"Never. My life is here, and I am content. I could be happy if you would agree to stay here with me as my wife."

"We'll see. You were young. You did what you had to. It doesn't compare."

"As you say, we'll see. Now it is your turn."

"When I left home I worked in the house of an English aristocrat in Boston. He wasn't in the country very often, but he had land and holdings here and so he visited for about three months of every year. However, he often allowed his friends to stay and use the house in his absence so there was always work to be done. I worked as a scullery maid. I was the lowest of the low and some of the male guests did not always behave as the gentlemen they were supposed to be." She stopped, unable to say exactly what they had done. But she could see the truth dawning on Mackenzie.

"They forced you?"

"Some of them did. One even professed to love me, wooed me and convinced me he would marry me and take me away with him. I fell pregnant. I believed it would all be resolved as he had said he loved me and could not live without me. But when I told him I never saw him again. Earl Lightfoot fired me on the spot, and I had to go home to the tenements where my poor Mama was dying of consumption. My sister was trying her best to bring up my brothers and sisters on the tiny wage I had sent home – but it was not enough and without it we were in dire straits indeed."

"What happened Annie? Because I see nothing that you have to be ashamed of. I see men who should have known better, men who took advantage of your youth and your kind soul. I see a world where the person most in need of care and support was the one cast out. None of that reflects badly on you."

"I sold my child! I sold my baby boy so I could get back to work, because I couldn't care for him!" she cried, unable to take any more of his kindness, his understanding.

"Oh Annie," he said tenderly as he pulled her to him and cradled her and let her sob. "You did what you had to do. Is your child well cared for? Does he want for anything?" She shook her head. "Then you did what was best for him. What more could you have done?"

"I should have found a way," she murmured.

"How old were you when this happened Annie?"

"I was fifteen."

"Oh my poor, poor girl. Such responsibility, such hardship to bear when you were so young. Like you so easily forgave me for my youth and foolishness – and I was in my early twenties when I was being so reckless with my life and those of others – I can forgive you anything. But, the problem is not my forgiveness is it? You can never forgive yourself, but you have to – for all the reasons you were able to forgive me. You were young and you had no choice. You did what you had to, in order to survive a brutal world. If I were still the pirate I used to be I'd be on my way to Boston to punish the men responsible."

"But don't all men want a virgin bride?"

"I could hardly judge you on terms of chastity. I chose to be unchaste – you were forced. How could I ever punish you for a sin I have committed myself. Your past is your past. You have no intentions of being unchaste once we are wed do you?"She shook her head. "Then you will marry me?"

"You sneak," she said her eyes lighting up. "You caught me. Yes, if you truly can forgive me I will marry you and the sooner the better!"

"Would you like me to see if we can have your son restored to you?"

"You would do that for me?" He nodded. "No, he is happy and

loved. It would break too many people's hearts to do so. But thank you for offering to do so. I do not deserve you."

"No Annie, it is I who do not deserve you – but maybe we can make a happy life together, a pair of old sinners!" He kissed her and she melted into his arms, glad to be free of her burden of guilt at last.

# Epilogue

The church in Great Falls was brimming with gardenias and lilies. The scent was intoxicating, but even more entrancing was the sight of his bride walking towards him on Carlton's arm. Mack had never been so happy in his entire life. Myra helped Annie to remove the veil from over her face and he was glad to see that she was wearing the self same excited grin he wore himself. She was truly beautiful, and kind and good. He would spend the rest of his life gladly making her happy.

"Do you Mackenzie Gladwin Stott take this woman to be your wife," the Minister intoned.

"I do, with all my heart," he replied.

"And do you Annie Cahill take this man to be your husband,"

"I do, gladly," she said solemnly.

"Then I now pronounce you man, and wife!" Without waiting for permission Mack lifted his bride and kissed her, not caring who was watching them – just knowing he had to claim her for his own forever and always.

Putting her down gently, they began to walk back down the aisle of the little chapel, and he took her hand in his. He felt a piece of paper in her hand. "What is this?" he asked as he took it from her and began to smooth out the wrinkles. A picture of a small boy stared back at him, his face alight with happiness. "Apparently they couldn't get him to look solemn," she said. "The photographer was apparently furious, was worried the exposure wouldn't come out right!"

"He is a handsome young man. I am glad he was here with you my love. And I have a surprise waiting for you at the ranch."

"A surprise? Whatever could you have been up to?" she asked impatiently.

"You shall have to wait," he teased. But no matter how much she tried to coax it from him he was not prepared to utter one word more. He lifted her up into the smart open carriage he had hired for the day and drove her back home. Waiting on the porch for her was her beloved sister and her two younger brothers. "I hope you don't mind, but I need some strong young men to help on the ranch, I figured you'd like it best if I could keep it in the family." She took his face in her palms and kissed him.

"You pirate, still kidnapping folk I see! Thank you. You will never know how much this means to me." He watched as she leapt out, her veil billowing behind her and was engulfed in the loving arms of her family. He was certain he knew exactly what it meant, because not having Penny by his side would have been, until now, the worst thing he could ever imagine. Now, the two orphaned families could become one happy, large one and that made him happier than he could ever have imagined too.

The End

Thank you for reading and supporting my book and I hope you enjoyed it.

Please will you do me a favor and leave a review so I'll know whether you liked it or not, it would be very much appreciated, thank you.

# Other books by Karla

**SUN RIVER BRIDES SERIES**

A bride for Carlton #1
A bride for Mackenzie #2
A bride for Ethan #3
A bride for Thomas #4
A bride for Mathew #5

# About Karla Gracey

Karla Gracey was born with a very creative imagination and a love for creating stories that will inspire and warm people's hearts. She has always been attracted to historical romance including mail order bride stories with strong willed women. Her characters are easy to relate to and you feel as if you know them personally. Whether you enjoy action, adventure, romance, mystery, suspense or drama- she makes sure there is something for everyone in her historical romance stories!